this
·little·barron's·
book belongs to

....

....

First edition for the United States and Canada published 1999 by
Barron's Educational Series, Inc.

Copyright © Nicola Smee 1999

First published in Great Britain by Orchard Books in 1999.

All inquiries should be addressed to:
Barron's Educational Series, Inc.
250 Wireless Boulevard, Hauppauge, New York 11788
http://www.barronseduc.com

Library of Congress Catalog Card No.: 98-74975
International Standard Book No. 0-7641-0872-7

Printed in Italy

9 8 7 6 5 4 3 2 1

Freddie Goes to
the Beach

Nicola Smee

• little • barron's •

Mom's taking Bear and me
to the beach! Hurray!

I can see the sea!
Bear can see the sea!
But I saw it first!

splish

splash

The sun is so hot Mom says we must put on sunscreen and sun hats so we don't burn.

I show Bear how to
make sandcastles.
(I learned at playschool.)
You need water to make
the sand stick!

We left the crab in the rock pool, but we're taking some seashells home to make a shell necklace for Mom.